P9-APN-333

Text copyright © 2006 by Antonio Ramírez
Illustrations copyright © 2006 by Domi
Translation copyright © 2006 by Groundwood Books

No part of this publication may be reproduced, stored in a
retrieval system or transmitted, in any form or by any means,
without the prior written consent of the publisher or a license
from The Canadian Copyright Licensing Agency (Access
Copyright). For an Access Copyright license, visit
www.accesscopyright.ca or call toll free to 1-800-893-5777.

Groundwood Books / House of Anansi Press
110 Spadina Avenue, Suite 801, Toronto, Ontario M5V 2K4
Distributed in the USA by Publishers Group West
1700 Fourth Street, Berkeley, CA 94710

Library and Archives Canada Cataloguing in Publication
Ramírez, Antonio
Napí goes to the mountain / story by Antonio Ramírez;
pictures by Domi; translated by Elisa Amado.
Translation of: Napí va a la montaña
ISBN-13: 978-0-88899-713-5
ISBN-10: 0-88899-713-2
1. Mazatec Indians–Juvenile fiction. I. Domi II. Amado, Elisa
III. Title.
PZ7.R16Na 2006   j863'.7   C2005-907881-2

The illustrations are in watercolor.

Printed and bound in China

To the boys and girls, children of landless farmers, the victims of capitalist greed — Antonio

To Paulino, my father, and Cirenia, my mother, with whom I lived through the adventure
of the founding of Nuevo Ixcatlán, my village, over half a century ago — Domi

Napí

Goes to the Mountain

ANTONIO RAMÍREZ

PICTURES BY

DOMI

TRANSLATED BY ELISA AMADO

GROUNDWOOD BOOKS
HOUSE OF ANANSI PRESS
TORONTO   BERKELEY

"Napí. Wake up, Napí. It's time for school," my mother said, shaking me gently.

I didn't want to open my eyes. "Has Namí come home yet?" I asked.

"No," she said quietly. "They are still out looking for him."

Namí didn't come home from working in the fields yesterday.
I saw his friends talking under the ceiba tree. They looked
worried. I crept over and pretended to throw stones in the river
so that I could hear what they were saying.

"Maybe the spirit Chicón dragged him off to his cave."
"No, he was probably bitten by a snake."
"Well, someone told me that he had seen some men hit him,
then take him away," said one man very quietly.

When he heard that, my grandfather chewed on his cigarette
and blew smoke out of his nose and mouth.

"It's because we've been fighting for our land. That's how
they treat us poor people when we won't bow down."

My grandfather was right. I know that's exactly what happens.
In the end, the men decided to go up into the mountain to
search for my namí.

So even though they had been searching all night, they still hadn't found him. I jumped out of bed, washed my face and hands and quickly ate some beans with tortilla and a little chile.

Then I put my things in my knapsack. But instead of going to school, I went down to the river to find my little brother, Niclé.

There's a raft down there that we like to jump off when we go swimming. My grandfather made it for us out of some jonote branches.

I began to untie the raft. "Come on, Niclé," I said. "We're going to look for Namí, okay?"

At first Niclé was excited, but then he looked serious.
"Okay," he said.

We picked up some little boards to use as paddles, jumped onto the raft and began to paddle upstream toward the mountain. But the current was so strong we were soon swirling around.

We lost our paddles and swept back down the river.
Niclé started to cry.
But a few seconds later he stopped, because we could both
feel the raft moving quickly and quietly up the river again.

It felt as though we were floating on air.

Niclé and I peered down curiously. We weren't even touching the water. Three turtles were carrying the raft on their backs! I noticed that one of them had a red rag tied around his foot.

Then I remembered. I'd found an injured turtle yesterday
and tied a piece of my red dress on his wound.
"That's the turtle I helped," I told Niclé.
The turtle looked up at me and winked.

We glided around one bend and then another until suddenly
we came upon Playa Shcuá, where the storks live. They perch
there in such big numbers that the trees all look white.

"Turtle friends," I said, "you can leave us here."
But they had already turned toward the beach.

We jumped ashore and I tied up the raft. Just as I was
hanging my knapsack on a branch, a white cloud of storks
wheeled around our heads, spinning and twirling us. We got so
dizzy that we fainted on the sand.

When I woke up, I leaped to my feet and pawed the sand.
Four feet? Suddenly I began to run and Niclé followed.

I looked at him and saw that he had little fawn antlers on his forehead and nice soft fur. Niclé was looking at me, and I realized that I had turned into a deer, too.

We walked softly through the jungle for a while. At the edge
of a stream we found a little coral snake lying very still.
"Little snake, please, have you seen our father?" we asked.

"Not near, not here," she hissed. "But when Chicón is ready,
you will find him. Walk on, walk on. You will find what you
seek." And she slithered into the undergrowth.

Every now and then a ray of sun pierced through the thick
leaves. It was fresh and new and beautiful in the jungle. My heart
beat fast with hope.

We jumped over one stream, then over the next and the next and the next. We lapped up some clear water to quench our thirst.

Then we found a bat sleeping in a cave.

He was hanging upside down with his little feet up in the air.

We woke him up.

"Little bat, please, have you seen our father?"

He pointed down at the ground with his wing. In a high squeaky voice he said, "He must be up there. I heard footsteps on my roof."

I didn't understand. He said up but he pointed down. Then I put my head between my legs so that I could see the world upside down like he did.

"Thank you, Mr. Bat," I said.

As we turned away we heard a faint mousy squeak. "Walk on, walk on. You will find what you seek."

We walked on and on, and then on and on.

We were so tired that we fell onto a pile of leaves. We rested there, warmed by a little patch of sun.

Just then a strange animal wearing beautiful armor trotted out of the jungle.

It was a mother armadillo. Her five babies came along right behind her.

"Mrs. Armadillo," said Niclé. "Can you tell us where our namí has gone?" But she paid no attention.

"Please, Mrs. Armadillo," I begged. But she said nothing as she walked by.

So I shouted, "Children! Little baby armadillos!" But on they went, without turning their heads, and popped down a tiny hole in the ground after their mother.

My brother and I looked at each other hopelessly. Our hearts were heavy. Then suddenly we heard a tiny whisper coming out of the hole.

"The family is finally together again."

And then there was silence except for the wind in the leaves.
"THE FAMILY IS FINALLY TOGETHER AGAIN!!!"
This time the armadillo shouted so loudly that the earth shook.

We jumped up as though we had been stung by thousands of ants.

"The mother armadillo is telling us that…" I began.

"…our namí is home again!" said Niclé.

"Thaaaank you, Mrs. Armadillo," we shouted together and —
jump, jump, jump — we leaped back the way we had come.

We crashed through the bushes onto Playa Shcuá. The sand
felt warm between my toes.

We were people again. I grabbed my knapsack and we
jumped onto the raft.

As we swept downstream, fishes, turtles, snails and shrimps
swam beside us.

They kept us company like brothers and sisters, children of the same mother, of the Earth.

When we reached our village we tied up our raft and ran home. Our father was happily drinking pozol with his friends.

It was so good to see him that I forgot to worry about where
he had been.

My mother walked over as soon as she saw us.
"Napí, did you go to school today?" she asked.
"No, Naá," I answered truthfully.
Because even though I love to dream, I never tell lies.

ceiba: large tropical tree from the Malvaceae family.

Chicón: name of a fearful spirit, Lord of the Earth.

jonote: tree from the Ficus family.

naá: mother in the Mazatec language.

namí: father in the Mazatec language.

Playa Shcuá: name of a beach. Shcuá means heron in
      the Mazatec language.

pozol: indigenous drink made from corn.